Biscuit
STORYBOOK FAVORITES

by Alyssa Satin Capucilli

pictures by Pat Schories

HARPER

An Imprint of HarperCollinsPublishers

Biscuit

by ALYSSA SATIN CAPUCILLI
pictures by PAT SCHORIES

This is Biscuit.

Biscuit is small.

Biscuit is yellow.

Time for bed, Biscuit!

Woof, woof!

Biscuit wants to play.

Time for bed, Biscuit!

Woof, woof!

Biscuit wants a snack.

Time for bed, Biscuit!

Woof, woof!

Biscuit wants a drink.

Time for bed, Biscuit!

Woof, woof!

Biscuit wants to hear a story.

Time for bed, Biscuit!

Woof, woof!

Biscuit wants his blanket.

Time for bed, Biscuit!

Woof, woof!

Biscuit wants his doll.

Time for bed, Biscuit!

Woof, woof!

Biscuit wants a hug.

Time for bed, Biscuit!

Woof, woof!

Biscuit wants a kiss.

Time for bed, Biscuit!

Woof, woof!

Biscuit wants a light on.

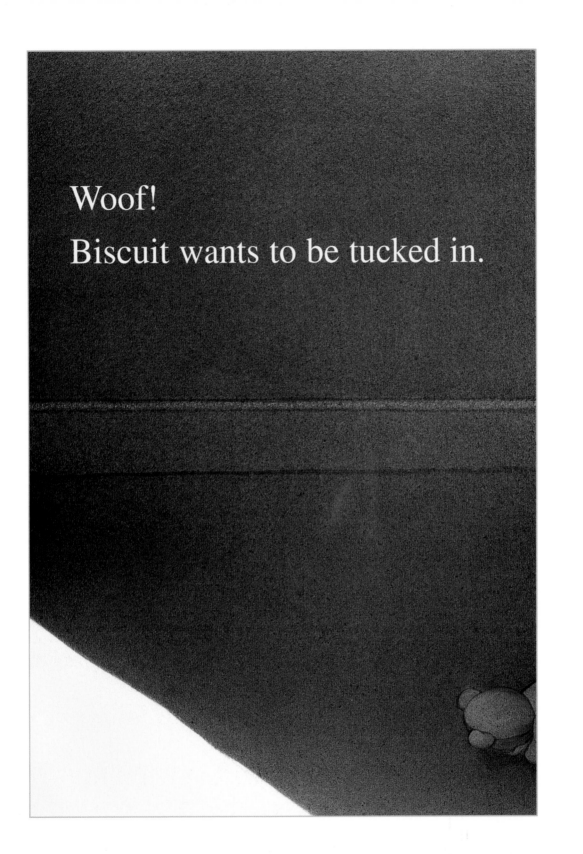

Woof!

Biscuit wants to be tucked in.

19

Woof!

Biscuit wants one more kiss.

Woof!

Biscuit wants one more hug.

Woof!

Biscuit wants to curl up.

Sleepy puppy.

Good night, Biscuit.

Biscuit
Wins a Prize

by ALYSSA SATIN CAPUCILLI • pictures by PAT SCHORIES

Here, Biscuit.

It's time for the pet show!

Woof, woof!

There will be lots of pets,
and prizes, too!
Woof, woof!

Come along, sweet puppy.

You want to look your best.

Woof!

Hold still, Biscuit.

Woof, woof!

Funny puppy! Don't tug now!

Hold still, Biscuit.

Woof, woof!

Oh, Biscuit!

It's not time to roll over.

Woof, woof!

It's time for the pet show!

Look at all the pets, Biscuit.

Woof, woof!

Biscuit sees his friend Puddles.

Bow wow!

Woof, woof!

Biscuit sees his friend Sam.

Ruff!

Woof, woof!

Biscuit sees
lots of new friends, too.

Woof, woof!

Hold still now, Biscuit.

Here comes the judge.

Woof!

Oh no, Biscuit. Come back!

Biscuit wants
to see the fish.
Woof!

Biscuit wants
to see the bunnies.
Woof!

Woof, woof!

Biscuit wants
to see all of the pets
at the pet show!

Silly puppy! Here you are.

What prize will you win now?

Woof, woof!

Oh, Biscuit!

You won the best prize of all!

Woof!

51

I Can Read!

SHARED
My
First
READING

Biscuit's New Trick

by ALYSSA SATIN CAPUCILLI

pictures by PAT SCHORIES

Here, Biscuit!

Look what I have.

Woof, woof!

It's time to learn

a new trick, Biscuit.

Woof, woof!

It's time to learn
to fetch the ball.
Ready?

Fetch the ball, Biscuit.

Woof, woof!

Silly puppy!

Don't roll over now.

Get the ball, Biscuit.

Fetch the ball, Biscuit.

Woof, woof!

Where are you going,
Biscuit?
Woof!

Funny puppy!
Fetch the ball,
not your bone.

Let's try again.

Fetch the ball, Biscuit!

Woof, woof!

Good puppy!

You got the ball.

Woof!

Wait, Biscuit.

Bring the ball back!

Woof, woof!

Let's try one more time.

Fetch the ball, Biscuit!

Woof, woof!

Oh no!
Not in the mud!

Stop, Biscuit!

Don't fetch it now!

Woof!

Oh, Biscuit!

You did it!

You learned a new trick!

Woof, woof!

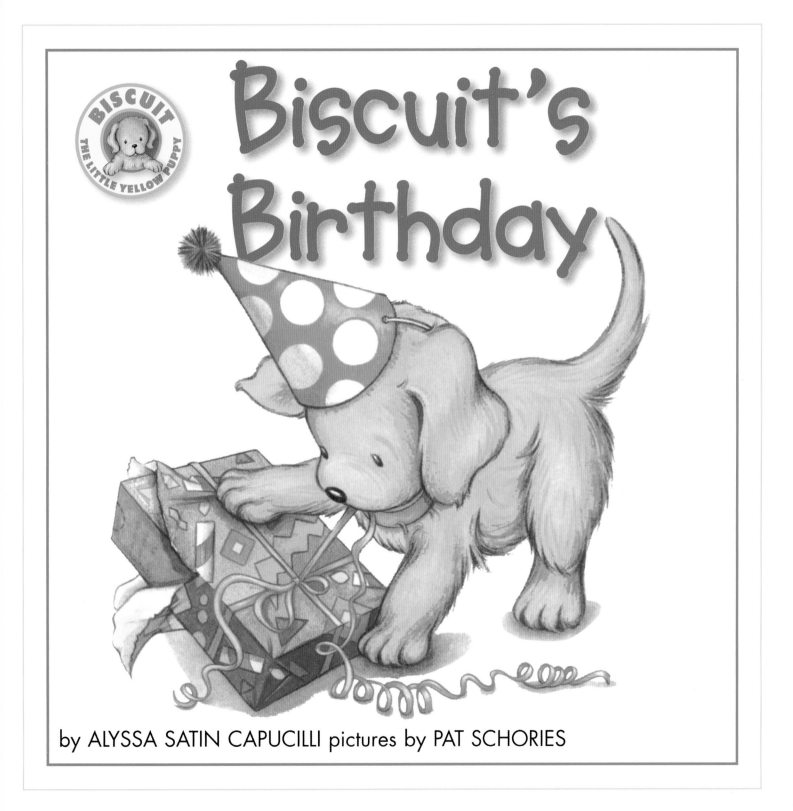

Biscuit's Birthday

by ALYSSA SATIN CAPUCILLI pictures by PAT SCHORIES

"Wake up, sleepy Biscuit!" said the little girl.
"Do you know what day it is?"
Woof!

"Today is a very special day.
It's your birthday!"
Woof! Woof!

"Follow me, Biscuit," said the little girl.
"I have something special planned just for you."

"Surprise, Biscuit! Puddles
and Daisy are here for your
birthday party!"

Bow wow!
Meow!

"Come along, everybody.
It's time to play some
birthday games."

Woof, woof!
Bow wow!
Meow!

"Silly Biscuit!" called the little girl.
"Be careful with those balloons."

"Oh, no," said the little girl. "There go the balloons!"
Woof!

"Oh, Biscuit!" The little girl laughed.
"You may be a year older, but you will
always be my silly little puppy."

"Now it's time for birthday treats,"
said the little girl.
"Make a wish, Biscuit."

Woof!

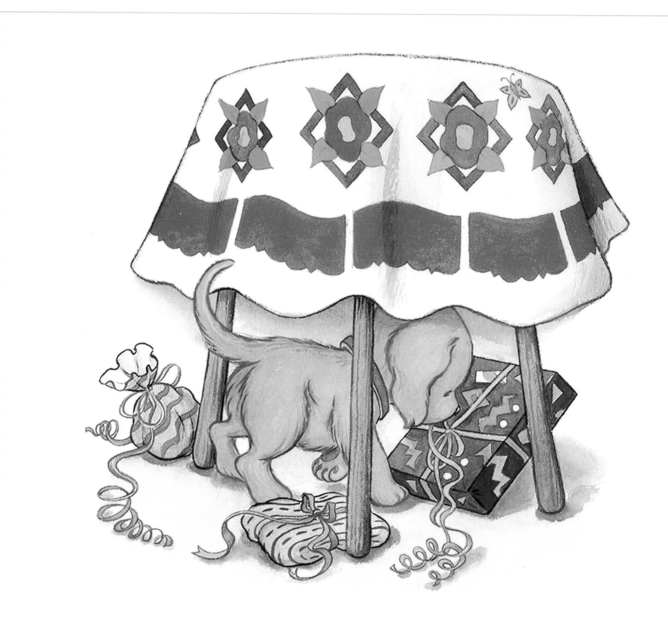

"Funny puppy! You want to open your birthday presents!"

"Look, Biscuit! A new collar, a new bone, and best of all . . ."

Woof, woof!

"A new box of biscuits!
Happy birthday, Biscuit!"

Woof!

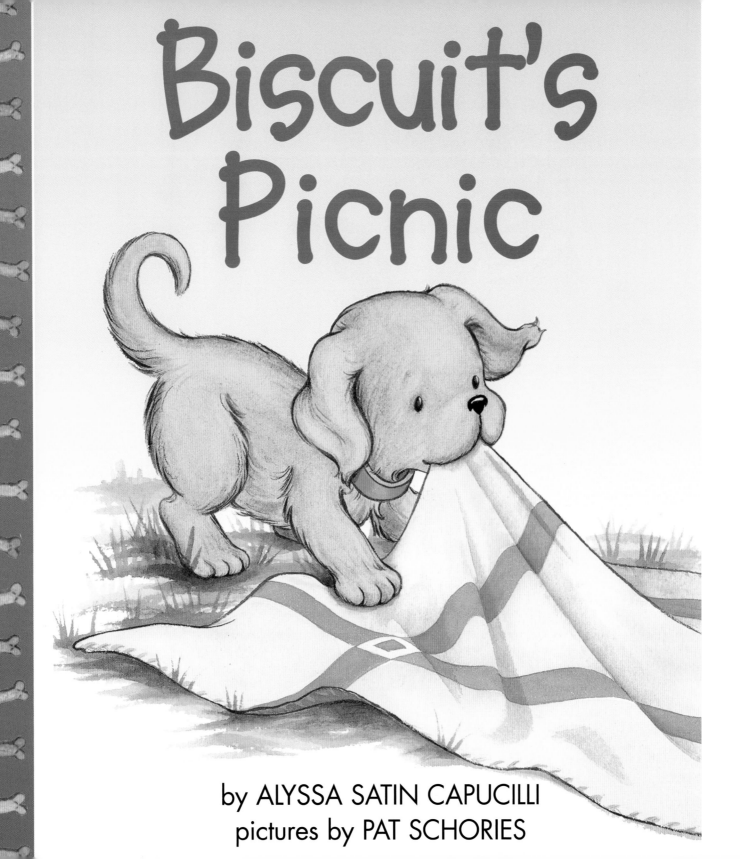

Biscuit's Picnic

by ALYSSA SATIN CAPUCILLI
pictures by PAT SCHORIES

"Biscuit, where are you?"
called the little girl.

Woof, woof!

"Silly puppy! What are you doing under there?"

Woof!

"I'm sorry, Biscuit. This picnic is just for kids.
You and Puddles can run and play."

Bow wow!

Woof, woof!

"Go on, puppies. Go and play!"

"Wait, Biscuit! Come back, Puddles!
Where are you going with that food?"

Tweet, tweet, tweet.
"Look!" The little girl laughed.
"Biscuit and Puddles are having
their own picnic—

and the birds want
to join them."

Bow wow!
Woof, woof, woof!

Meow.

"Even Daisy wants to have a picnic!"

Meow.

Woof, woof!

Bow wow, bow wow!

"Careful, Biscuit!" said the little girl.
"Watch out for the—

—CAKE!"

"Biscuit is covered in cake!"
the little boy giggled.
"Oh, Biscuit," said the little girl.
"What do we do now?"

Woof, woof!

"Funny puppy. You're right, Biscuit," she said.
"We can all have a picnic together!"

Woof!

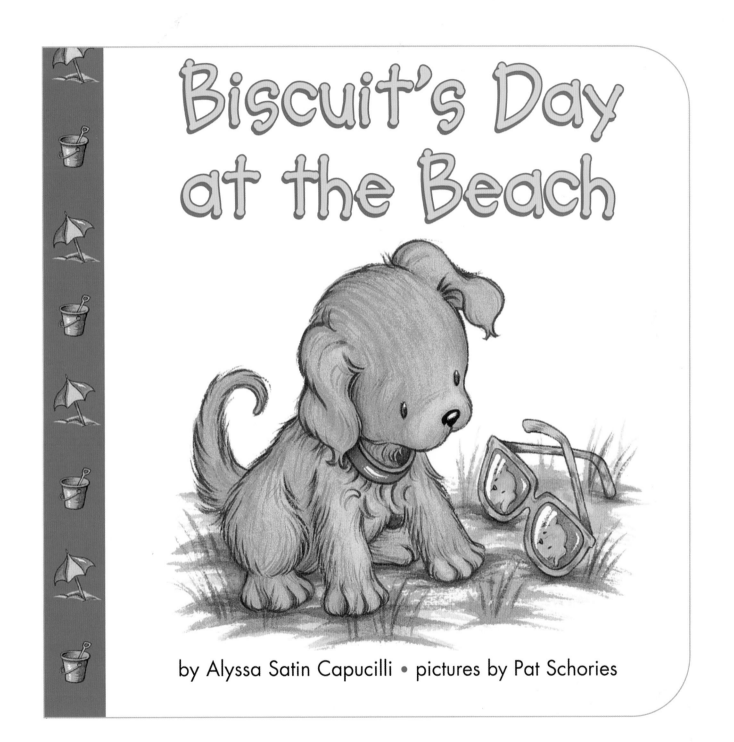

Biscuit's Day at the Beach

by Alyssa Satin Capucilli • pictures by Pat Schories

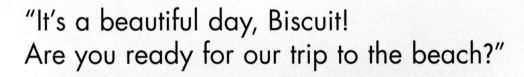

"It's a beautiful day, Biscuit!
Are you ready for our trip to the beach?"

Woof, woof!

"Me, too! Let's go!"

"It's fun to have a picnic at the beach.
Let's pack some sandwiches."

Woof, woof!

"Silly puppy!
How did you get those biscuits?"

"We'll need pails and shovels."

Woof, woof!

"Funny puppy!
Come out of there!"

"Come on, Daisy.
You can come to the beach, too."

Meow!

Woof, woof!

Bow wow!

"Look, Biscuit! It's Puddles!"

Woof, woof!

Quack!

"Even the little duck wants to visit the beach!
All we need now is a cool ocean breeze."

Woof, woof!

"Oh, no, Biscuit! Not a big shake!
Silly puppy!"

"There's nothing like a day at the beach, is there, Biscuit?"

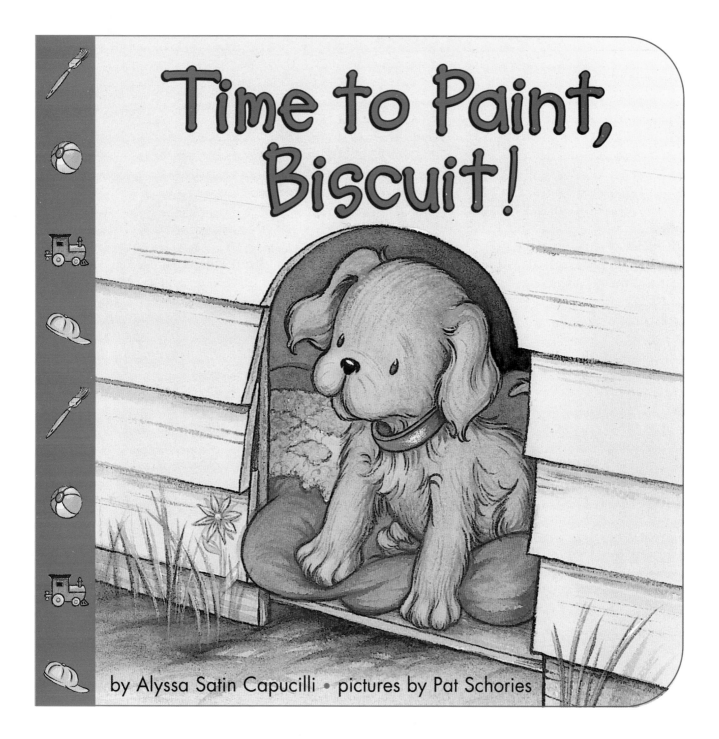

Time to Paint, Biscuit!

by Alyssa Satin Capucilli • pictures by Pat Schories

"Come along, Biscuit!
Spring is here at last!"

Woof, woof!

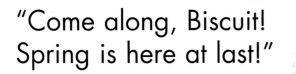

"We can play later, little puppy.
First, we have some spring cleaning to do!"

Woof!

"It's time to paint your doghouse, Biscuit.
Just look at what's inside!"

Woof, woof!

Quack!

"Sleepy little duck!
It's time to come out now!
Spring is here!"

"Here are the paintbrushes and the paint. Now we're ready to get started."

Woof, woof!

"And here are some friends to help us!"

Bow wow!

"Hello, Puddles!"

"A fresh coat of paint is just what your doghouse needs, Biscuit.
This yellow paint is shiny and bright."

Woof, woof!

Bow wow!

"Silly puppies!
No playing near the paint!"

"Now it's time for the red paint.

B – I – S – C – U – I – T

There, Biscuit! Your doghouse is
as good as new!"

Woof, woof!

"Funny puppy.
You want to paint, too!"

"Oh, no, Biscuit! Watch out for the wet paint!"

Woof, woof!

Bow wow!

"Sweet puppy!
You knew just what your doghouse
really needed!"

Woof, woof!

Biscuit Meets the Neighbors

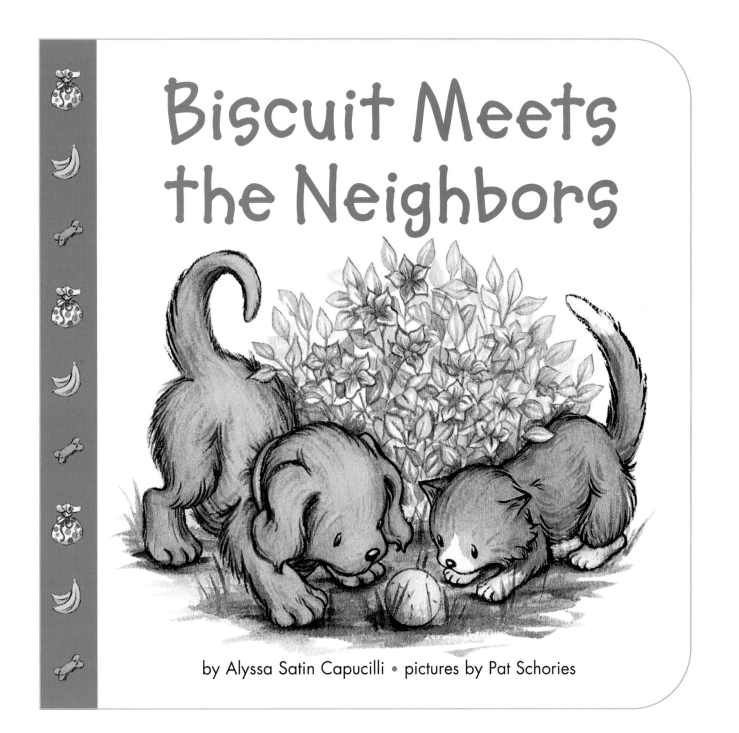

by Alyssa Satin Capucilli • pictures by Pat Schories

"Look, Biscuit!
Look, Daisy!
Our new neighbors are moving in today!"

Meow!
Woof, woof!

"Let's bring a basket of goodies
to welcome them.
Oh, no!
That basket is not for you!"

"I can hardly wait to meet our new neighbors.
Biscuit! Daisy!
This is no time for digging!"

"Silly puppy!
Funny kitty!
You want to bring flowers along!"

153

Meow!
Woof, woof!

"Oh, Biscuit and Daisy!
You found a ball...

. . . and you found ou

new neighbors, too!"

"Sweet Biscuit!
Sweet Daisy!
It looks like we've all made new
friends today!"

Meow!

Woof, woof!

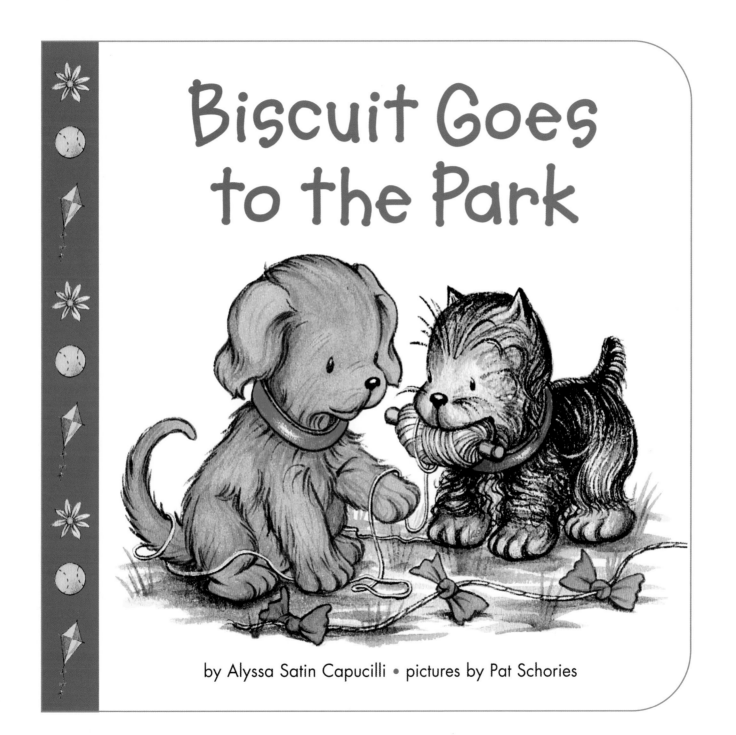

Biscuit Goes
to the Park

by Alyssa Satin Capucilli • pictures by Pat Schories

"Here, Biscuit!
I have a surprise for you!"

Woof, woof!

"Puddles is here!"

"We're all going to the park!"

Bow wow!
Woof, woof!

"Biscuit! Puddles!
Wait for us!"

"Funny puppies!
You want to chase the birds and butterflies!"

Bow wow!
Woof, woof!

"And you want to chase the kites, too!"

Bow wow!

Woof, woof!

"Come back, Biscuit!
Come back, Puddles!"

"Oh, no!
That's not your kite.
Whose kite can it be?"

172

"Sweet puppies!
You found the kite and our friends."

Bow wow!
Woof, woof!

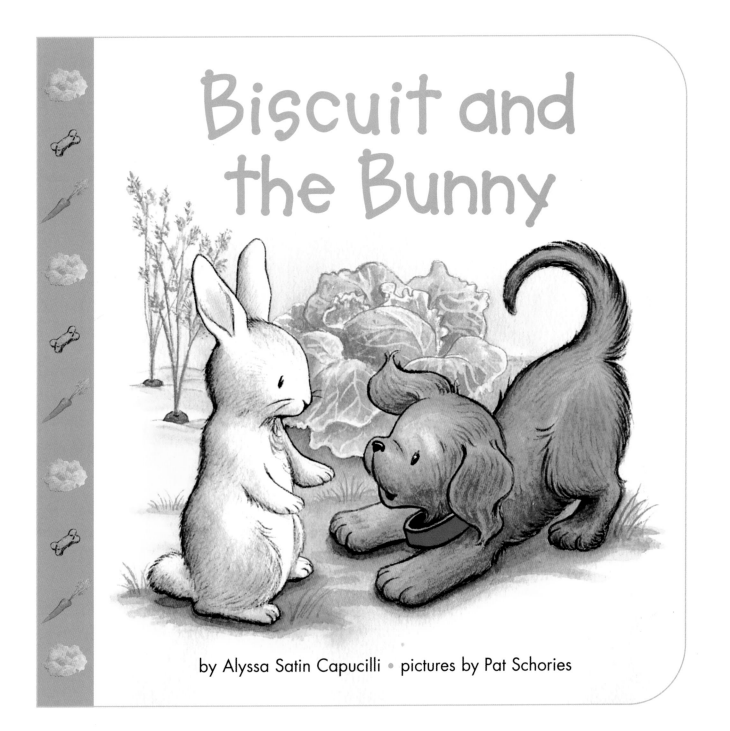

Biscuit and the Bunny

by Alyssa Satin Capucilli • pictures by Pat Schories

Woof, woof!

"Here, Biscuit!
What have you found?"

Woof, woof!

"Look, Biscuit.
It's a bunny!"

"Silly puppy.
Don't be shy."

Woof, woof!

"Good puppy!
That's the way!"

"See, Biscuit.
Bunnies like lettuce and carrots."

Woof, woof!

"The bunny likes your doll!"

Woof, woof!

"We can name the bunny Dolly."

"Dolly likes your blanket, too!"

Woof, woof!

"Sweet puppy.
You always know how to share."

Hop! Hop!
Woof, woof!

"Oh, Biscuit!
It's always fun to make a new friend."

Woof!

Woof, woof!

Bow wow!

HARPER
An Imprint of HarperCollinsPublishers
www.harpercollinschildrens.com
Illustrations © Pat Schories